For Anna
M.W.

For Sebastian,
David & Candlewick
H.O.

First published by Candlewick Press

CANDLEWICK PRESS
2067 MASSACHUSETTS AVENUE
CAMBRIDGE MA 02140

ISBN 0-590-62153-X

Text copyright © 1991 by Martin Waddell.
Illustrations copyright © 1991 by Helen Oxenbury.

12 11 10 9 8 7 6 5 4 3 2 1   5 6 7 8 9/9 0/0

Printed in the U.S.A.   08

First Scholastic printing, October 1995

FARMER DUCK

by
MARTIN WADDELL

illustrated by
HELEN OXENBURY

CANDLEWICK PRESS
CAMBRIDGE, MASSACHUSETTS

There once was a duck
who had the bad luck to live
with a lazy old farmer.
The duck did the work.
The farmer stayed
all day in bed.

The duck fetched the cow from the field.

"How goes the work?" called the farmer.

The duck answered,

"Quack!"

The duck brought the sheep from the hill.

"How goes the work?" called the farmer.

The duck answered,

"Quack!"

The duck put the hens in their house.

"How goes the work?"

called the farmer.

The duck answered,

"Quack!"

The farmer got fat through staying in bed,

and the poor duck got fed up

with working all day.

"How goes the work?"

"Quack!"

"How goes the work?"

"Quack!"

"How goes the work?"

"Quack!"

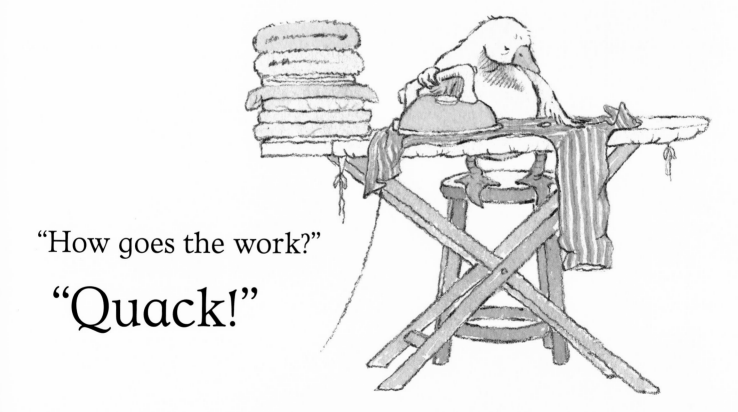

"How goes the work?"

"Quack!"

"How goes the work?"

"Quack!"

"How goes the work?"

"Quack!"

Soon, the poor duck grew
sleepy and weepy
and tired.

The hens and the cow and the
sheep got very upset.
They loved the duck.
So they held a meeting under
the moon, and they made
a plan for the morning.

"Moo!"

said the cow.

"Baa!"

said the sheep.

"Cluck!"

said the hens.

And *that* was the plan!

It was just before dawn and the farmyard was still.
Through the back door and into the house
crept the cow and the sheep
and the hens.

They stole
down the hall.
They creaked
up the stairs.

They squeezed under the bed of
the farmer and wriggled about.
The bed started to rock
and the farmer woke up,
and he called
"How goes the work?"
and…

"Moo!"

"Baa!"

"Cluck!"

They lifted his bed
and he started to shout,
and they banged and they bounced
the old farmer about and about and about,
right out of the bed...

and he fled with the cow and the sheep and the hens

mooing and baaing and clucking behind him.

Down the lane…

"Moo!"

through the fields…

"Baa!"

over the hill…

'Cluck!"

and he never came back.

The duck awoke and he waddled wearily into the yard expecting to hear, "How goes the work?" But nobody spoke!

Then the cow and the sheep
and the hens came back.

"Quack?" asked the duck.

"Moo!" said the cow.

"Baa!" said the sheep.

"Cluck!" said the hens.

Which told the duck
the whole
story.

Then mooing and baaing
and clucking and quacking,
they all set to work
on their farm.